I'm NOT SCARED

Published by Bonney Press,
an imprint of Hinkler Books Pty Ltd
45–55 Fairchild Street
Heatherton Victoria 3202 Australia
www.hinkler.com.au

BONNEY
PRESS

Author: Dan Crisp
Illustrator: Lee Wildish
Prepress: Graphic Print Group

ISBN: 978 1 7436 3500 1

Printed and bound in China

I'm NOT SCARED

Dan Crisp   Lee Wildish

I'm not scared of MONSTERS. They don't frighten me.

Even ones with scary eyes;

I'd let them
dine with me!

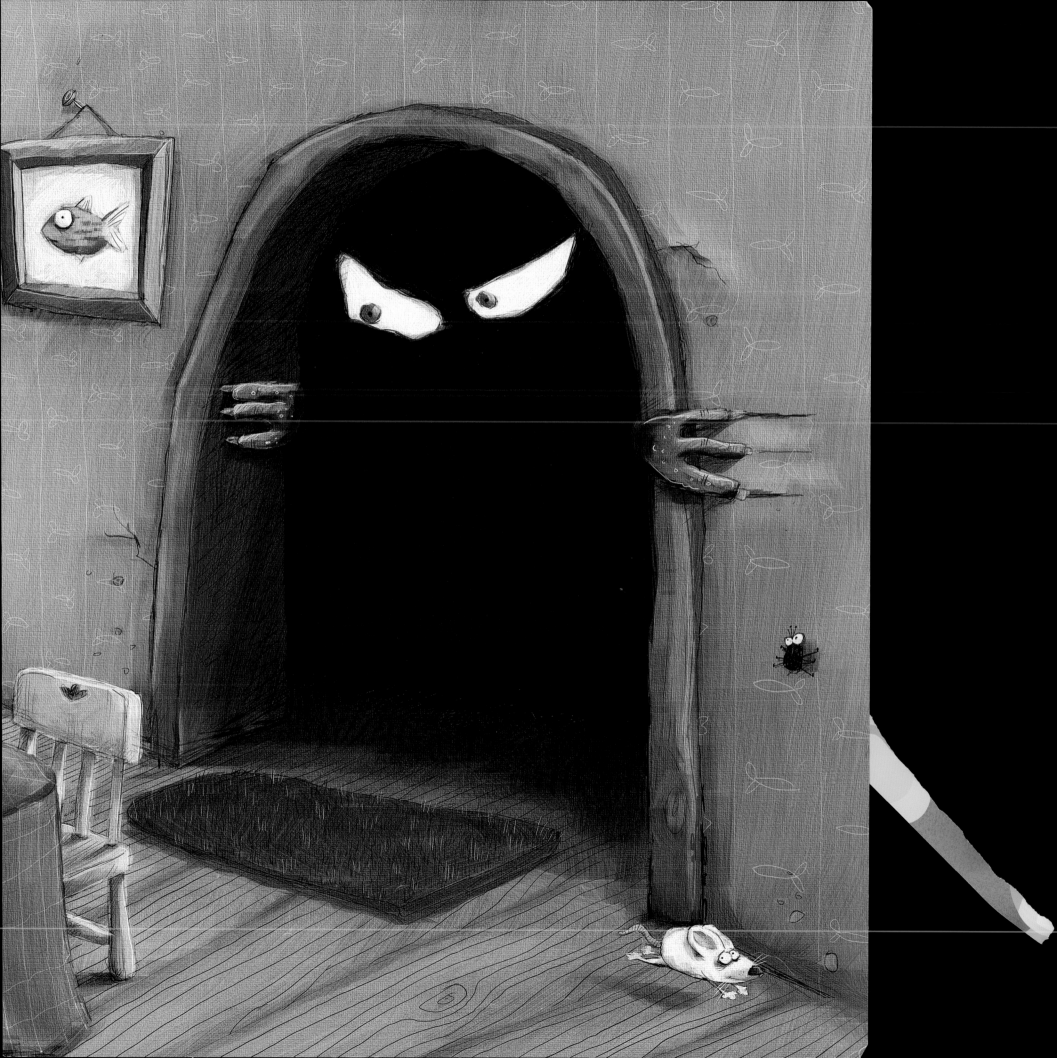

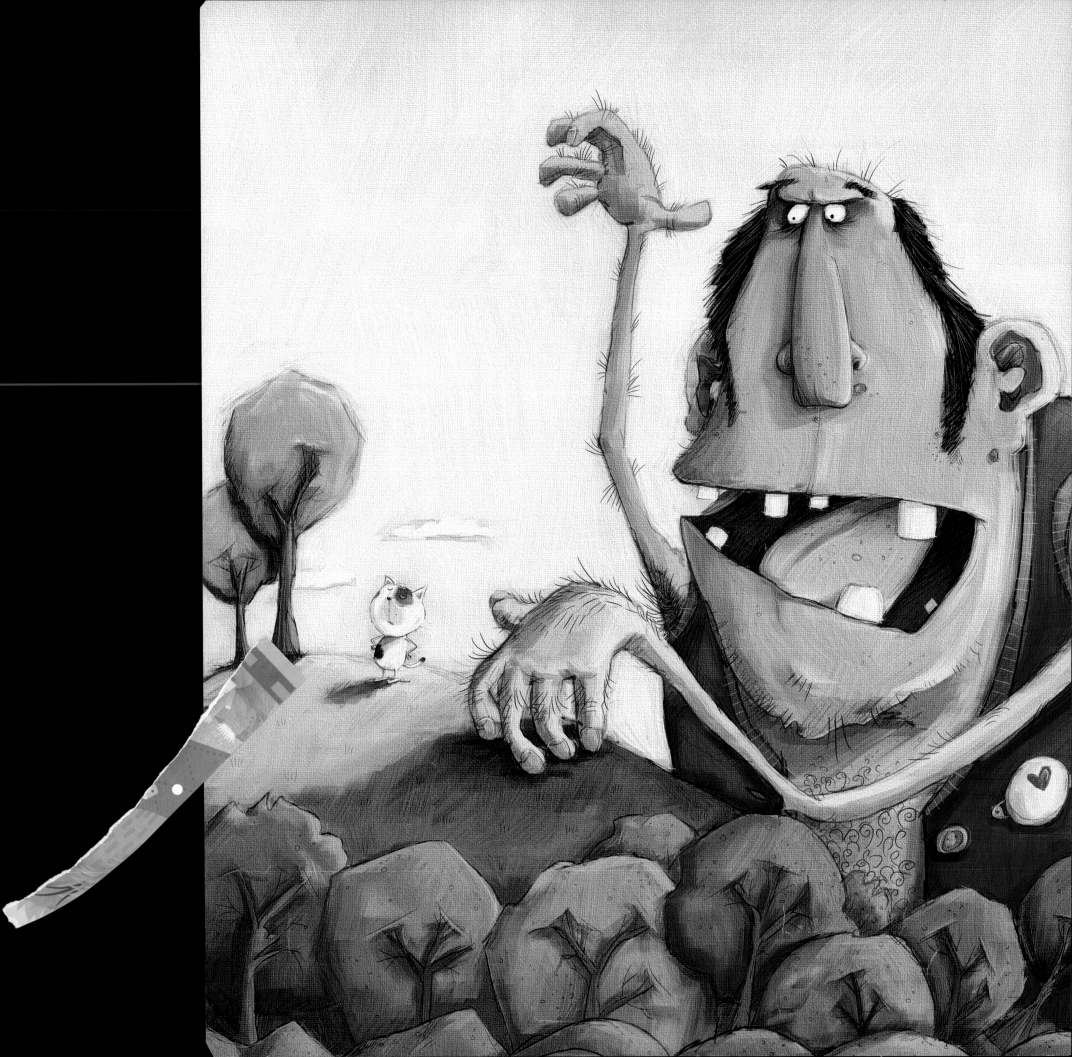

I'm not scared of GIANTS,

hanging out in the wild.

Even if they're man-eating beasts, and I am just a child.

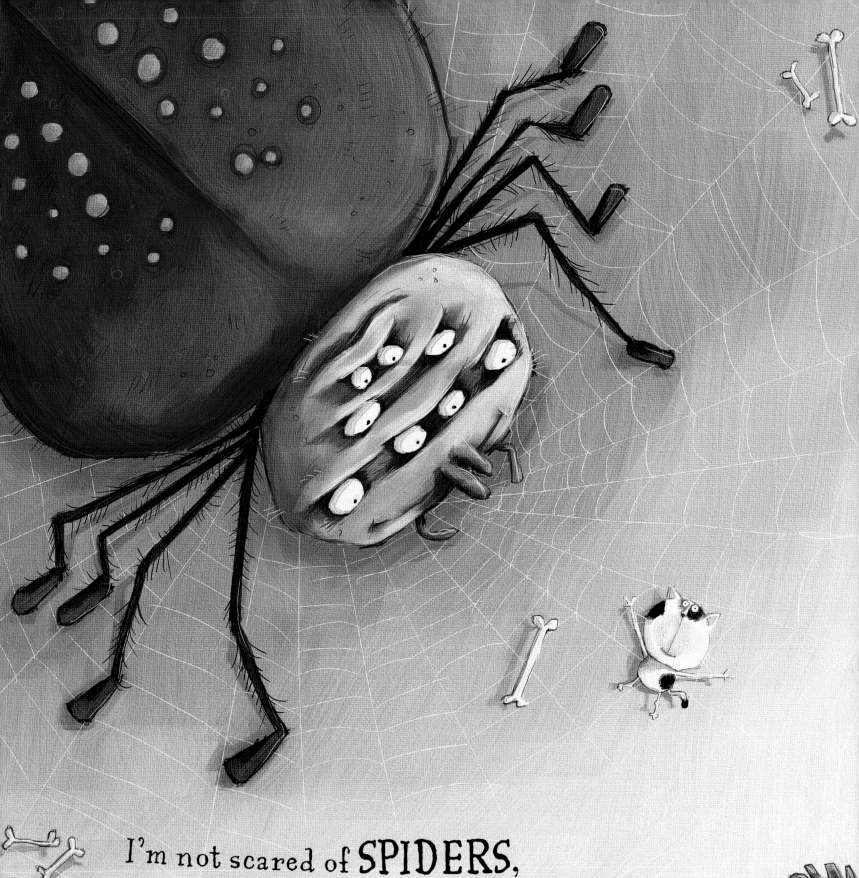

I'm not scared of SPIDERS,
be they as big as a bus.

Cornered by a crowd of
CROCS,
I wouldn't make a fuss.

I'm even fine with WITCHES, as evil as they can be.

GHOSTS, GHOULS and VAMPIRES –

they don't frighten me!

I'm not scared of SKELETONS,

rattling all their bones.

Or strange sounds from the cellar;
the creepy moans and groans.

I'm not scared of OGRES and their great big beady eyes.

Lurking under bridges; they can't make me cry.

The
lions

and the
tigers,

great **grizzly bears** too.

They don't scare me **one little bit**...

how about you?

I'm not scared of JELLYFISH,

SHARKS or

WRIGGLING EELS.

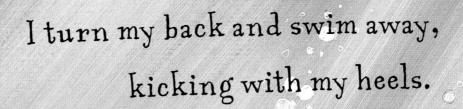

I turn my back and swim away,

kicking with my heels.

I'm not afraid of DRAGONS,

with their fire and scaly skin.

ROARING, *SCREAMING* and jumping about –

all I do is grin.

You'll have to please excuse me;
there's someone at the door . . .